Can I slurp my SPAGHETTI?

This book belongs to

....

THIS STORY HAS...

Jessie's Dad

Jessie
She lives with her
mum, dad and
Baby Archie

**Jessie's
mummy**

Archie
Jessie's baby brother

Charlie
Jessie's friend

Alfie
Jessie's friend

Amelia
Jessie's friend

Read more books in this series:

Where are you Scruffy Pup?

My Turn, Your Turn

Swim Like A Fish

CAN I SLURP MY SPAGHETTI?

A LAUGHING LOBSTER BOOK 978-1-913906-96-2
Published in Great Britain by Laughing Lobster, an imprint of Centum Publishing Ltd.
This edition published 2021.

5 7 9 10 8 6 4

Illustrations by Julia Seal.

Laughing Lobster, an imprint of Centum Publishing Ltd, 20 Devon Square, Newton Abbot, Devon, TQ12 2HR, UK. Centum Publishing Ltd, 9/10 Fenian St, Dublin 2, D02 RX24, Ireland

books@centumpublishingltd.co.uk

LAUGHING LOBSTER, CENTUM PUBLISHING LIMITED Reg. No. 08497203

A CIP catalogue record for this book is available from the British Library.

Printed in Great Britain.

FSC
www.fsc.org
MIX
Paper from
responsible sources
FSC® C014540

Can I slurp my SPAGHETTI?

Let's play hide and seek! Can you find this bird hiding in the story 9 times?

"Yippee!"
Jessie kicked off her covers, then jumped up and down on the bed. Today was a very exciting day. Her best friends were coming to tea!

"When will Charlie and the twins get here?" asked Jessie. "Is it soon?"
"Steady on," chuckled Mum. "You haven't had breakfast yet."

As soon as she'd got dressed, Jessie rushed downstairs.
"Hello Dad!" she called. "Did you make my favourite tea?"
"Yes," smiled Dad. "The spaghetti's in the fridge, all
ready for later."

Jessie gave Dad a big hug. Her little brother Archie
clapped his hands. Jessie and Archie loved spaghetti!

"Time for work," said Dad, grabbing a slice of toast. "Have fun with your friends. Oh, and save some spaghetti for me!"

"Charlie can sit here," decided Jessie, "Alfie can go there and Amelia can sit next to me."

"Archie?" said Archie.

"Only big boys and girls can sit at the table," said Jessie. "You must go in your high chair."

Jessie went to the Little Caterpillars Nursery. She ran up to the front door.
"There's Alfie and Amelia!" she cried, waving at them.

Charlie was waiting.

"Hello!" he said. "I'm coming to your house today."

Jessie nodded. Archie tried to get out of his buggy.

"No Archie," said Jessie. "Only big boys and girls go to nursery."

Nursery was brilliant.

Jessie and her
friends played
musical instruments,

wiggled their fingers
in the water tray,

and made twisty
train tracks.

When their helper, Jenny, started the goodbye song, Amelia grinned. Alfie and Charlie wriggled on their chairs. It was time to go to tea at Jessie's house!

"This is our playroom," said Jessie, when all her friends had arrived.

"What shall we play?" asked Alfie.

"Let's build a tower," cried Charlie.

Jessie and Alfie fetched the bricks. Amelia and Charlie
built them up and up and up.

Crash!

Archie knocked the tower down to the ground.

Jessie and her friends tried again.
"This new tower is going to reach the ceiling," said Alfie.
The tower got taller and taller and taller until…

Crash! Archie knocked it down all over again!

"Mum!" shouted Jessie. "Archie keeps spoiling
our game."
"Never mind," said Mum. "It's time for tea."

Everybody washed their hands and sat down. Mum put Archie in his high chair.

Charlie stared at his bowl.

"What's that?"

Jessie smiled. "It's my dad's spaghetti. It's the best!"

"It looks like worms," said Charlie, pushing his bowl away.

"I don't want it. I never eat spaghetti at my house."

Alfie and Amelia pushed their bowls away, too.

Jessie felt sad. Her special tea had all gone wrong. "Come on, Charlie," Jessie's mum said, gently. "Jessie's dad has made this especially – he'll be upset if you don't at least try a little bit."
Charlie felt sad.

Slurpppppp!

Archie sucked up
a curly-wurly string
of spaghetti. Jessie frowned.
"You mustn't slurp your
spaghetti, Archie," she sighed.

Charlie looked at Alfie and then Amelia. Alfie and Amelia both put spaghetti onto their forks. Then Charlie put a teeny tiny piece of spaghetti on his fork.

Slurp!
Slurpp!
Slurppppp!

Charlie slowly sucked up the spaghetti. So did Alfie, so did Amelia.

"Mmm . . ." said Alfie. "It tastes nice."

"It's really, really nice!" giggled Amelia.

"I love it!" said Charlie.

Jessie and her friends ate everything up.
"What lovely clean bowls!" said Mum.
"Can we come again?"
asked Charlie.

Jessie gave Archie a kiss.
"Sometimes even big boys and girls are allowed to
slurp their spaghetti," she decided, "just a little bit!"

THE END

✳ CAN YOU REMEMBER?

Who makes Jessie's favourite tea and what is it?

Where does Jessie go before her friends come round for tea?

Who comes round to Jessie's house?

Who knocks down the tower
they all build?

What does Charlie say the
spaghetti looks like?

Slurpppppp!

How do they all eat
their spaghetti?

SAY GOODBYE TO...

Jessie's Dad

Jessie
She lives with her mum, dad and Baby Archie

Jessie's mummy

Archie

Jessie's baby brother

Charlie

Jessie's friend

Alfie

Jessie's friend

Amelia

Jessie's friend

HOPE YOU ENJOYED
THE STORY!